Don't Blame Me!

Written by Charlotte Guillain

Illustrated by Jon Stuart

Collins

Chimp sat in a tree. He liked to eat mangoes.

But when he had eaten the mangoes,
he liked to throw the skins away.

One day, a mango skin fell right over Snake! Splat!

4

Snake got a fright. "Oh no!" she hissed.
"I cannot see!" She slithered away into
a hole.

Polecat was sitting inside the hole.
He jumped up in fright.

Polecat landed on Snake's back and went for a ride!

When Ostrich spotted Polecat and Snake,
she was amazed!

Ostrich was so shocked, she laid an egg as big as a boulder!

The egg started to roll down the hill.
It plopped into the lake!

The big splash woke up Gecko, and he jumped in fright!

11

Gecko smacked right into Hippo's shoulder!
Hippo was so shocked she started bellowing.

Hippo's bellowing frightened a herd of buffaloes. They panicked!

The buffaloes thundered across to the trees.
They woke up Chimp.

The tree started to shake, and Chimp fell out. "What's going on?" he yelled.

"Don't blame us!" said the buffaloes.
"It was Hippo!"

Hippo frowned at Gecko. "Don't blame me!" said Hippo. "Gecko smacked into my shoulder!"

"Don't blame me!" yelled Gecko.
"Ostrich's egg frightened me!"

"Don't blame me!" honked Ostrich.
She frowned at Polecat.

"Don't blame me!" said Polecat.

"Snake came into my hole!"
squeaked Polecat.

"A mango skin fell on me!" hissed Snake.

"Oh no!" said Chimp. "I will never throw mango skins again!"

And he never did!

Can you name all the animals
Chimp upsets?

 After reading

Letters and Sounds: Phase 5

Word count: 249

Focus phonemes: /ai/ ay, ey, a-e /ee/ ea /igh/ i, i-e /oa/ o, oe, ow, ou, o-e

Common exception words: me, she, he, what, said, my, out, was, to, when, the, oh, into, of, you, all, one

Curriculum links: Science: Animals, including humans; PSHCE

National Curriculum learning objectives: Reading/word reading: read accurately by blending sounds in unfamiliar words containing GPCs that have been taught; read words containing taught GPCs; Reading/comprehension: understand both the books they can already read accurately and fluently and those they listen to by checking that the text makes sense to them as they read, and correcting inaccurate reading

Developing fluency

- Your child may enjoy hearing you read the book.
- Take turns to read a page. Check that your child uses a variety of tones, such as extra emphasis for exclamations and different voices for the animals.

Phonic practice

- Focus on spellings of /oa/ and /ow/ sounds. Ask your child to sound out:

  down   bellow   frowned   throw

- Look together at page 15. Ask your child to find the word with the /oa/ sound. (**going**)

Extending vocabulary

- Look at pages 8 and 9 and ask your child to think of another word with a similar meaning (synonym) for each of the following:

  spotted (e.g. *noticed, saw*)   shocked (e.g. *startled, surprised*)
  amazed (e.g. *astonished, astounded*)

- Take turns to choose a word for the other to think of a synonym.